Alt-Future

QueenSpark Publishers
Brighton & Hove

First published 2006

QueenSpark Publishers is a non-profit community publishing and writing organisation, which for over thirty years has helped the people of Brighton & Hove to tell their stories.

Find out more about QueenSpark at www.queensparkbooks.org.uk

QueenSpark Publishers, 49 Grand Parade, Brighton, BN2 2QA.
Tel. 01273 571710

ISBN 0-904733-47-5

A catalogue record of this book is available from the British Library

Edited and designed by Peter Oakes

ARTS COUNCIL ENGLAND

Contents

Introduction

Alt-Future is a companion to 2005's *Alt-History*, which invited people to create fictional histories of Brighton & Hove. Inspired by the response to that initiative – both from those who entered stories and those who subsequently read them – QueenSpark embarked upon a similar path for this book: a competition was advertised locally and via our website, inviting creative and imaginative contributions from adults and young people on the future of the city. Alongside the competition we ran a writing course, for those who needed support to develop ideas into coherent stories.

This book continues QueenSpark's commitment to the development of local writing; coinciding with its publication, we are launching ***www.thedeckchair.org.uk*** a literary website for Brighton & Hove, which will enable people to submit articles, features, stories and reviews for editorial feedback, and online publication.

QueenSpark's congratulations go to Josie Darling and Charli Gunn, who won the adult's and young people's competitions respectively, and whose stories are featured first and second in this anthology. Our thanks also go to Sheila McWattie, John McPherson and Linda Verrall, who gave valuable editorial feedback to some of the writers.

Happy reading.

John Riches
Director
QueenSpark Publishers

Alt-Future

Msg 28.11.2046

Josie Darling

MUM

28
11
204
6

9
204
11
28
28
11
204
6

9
204
11
28
28
11
204
6

RUOK?

Soz L8 writin. Bton uni iz cool, me appy
Da yurt me liv in iz wicked. Warm wiv sola panel.
Ave taken all erbs, no m8s wiv disease

No probs wiv veg. We work Churchill square
alotmence evry day. Me best m8 croydon
cooks afta yoga. The yoga centas called
escape, afta nite club in old days. Me hemp clothes
need wash.

Did u c news bout kid who got smacked
by him mum ? Bad huh.Police caught boy smokin
cig ere yest. Like da dark ages man.

Ave job mindin ome educated kids, most ere do not do skool .
We lost r identity cards man, C life centa not let us in.

Twoz King Fat Boy Slims funeral las week.
Da street lined wiv all the People from da city
- all 16-25. Da tube from London packed 2.

Soz mum u cant visit cos you ova 25
I will cum c u in Woodingdean.

Luv u mum

Portslade x

Josie Darling *I was born in 1969 in the house in Winchester where Jane Austen died, and lived there and in Yarmouth, Isle of Wight. I met me partner Danny when we were seventeen, and when I was nineteen, after living in a caravan for a year, I moved to London to train to be a nurse. I had my first baby in 1992. I moved to Brighton in 1993, where I have been nursing in a hospice and having babies (four altogether) ever since.*
I'm keen on growing veg, writing lists, my improvisation group and going to bed early. We have four pets: hamster, cat, dog and horse.

DIY History
Charli Gunn

'Class dismissed.'

The words sounded like a blessing, even in the strange, cheese-grater voice of the Year 7 History Teaching Module, known as 7HT or Sir for short. The pupils charged through the door, eager to get home and wash off that first-day-at-school reek. Sparrow, not as enthusiastic as the others about leaving school, slouched along more slowly. History was her favourite subject, and the lesson had been particularly interesting. She only wished it could have gone on longer.

She had learnt that her name, Sparrow, was a type of bird that died out in the 2090s. The last one had died in 2098, the year, month, week, day she had been born, hence her name. And also the Pavilion, the popular floating restaurant-in-the-sky, had once been a house called a palace for a person called a Prince in the days when there were people called Kings and Queens ruling the country instead of a Computer Government.

The second Sparrow left the school gates, the HoverBus revved up and zoomed away over the city.

Great. I've missed the bus again. Sparrow thought, as she kicked at nothing in particular.

She sighed, and began the long walk home.

As she walked, Sparrow pondered the times before humans had polluted the Earth.

DIY History lesson, step one. she thought, grinning to herself, glad for very, *very* definitely the first time that her father had gone and implanted that stupid, cranky computer-chip in her skull. Sparrow glanced about the mostly deserted street and, as casually as possible, ducked into an alleyway.

'Search Brighton landmarks from 2000 to 2025.' Sparrow commanded, enunciating as clearly as was possible while barely moving her lips.

'Searching... Searching...' stated a voice in her head.

Well get on with it! Sparrow muttered as loud as she dared. The minute computer could occasionally pick up on stray thoughts and malfunction. Of course, the professional computer-chips that rich people could buy were properly thought-operational, had a search time of less then 1.265 microseconds and *NEVER* malfunctioned. Blow her dad for doing DIY with her head.

Tapping her foot impatiently, Sparrow heard the machine deadpan; 'Search complete. Six file[s] found. Qualification - three text, three image.'

Trying to remember some of the more complex commands for the chip, Sparrow asked tentatively, 'Compare equivalent landmarks, 2109.'

She breathed a sigh of relief as the machine whirred into action, the little voice in her head twittering 'Comparing...' all the while.

As Sparrow went over the third, more complex, command in her mind. The unit's voice announced, 'Files evaluated.'

'Open files, voice over narration of corresponding text.' Sparrow commanded.

Her vision blurred, and then sharpened to reveal two pictures about the size of a 'postcard' she'd seen in a museum recently.

'Brighton... Pavilion... 2005. A palace for a prince, the son of the King and Queen, who ruled the country,' the voice purred, 'Brighton... Pavilion... 2109.' it continued, '...Flying restaurant, popular with children – owned by Ferdinand Todd, who bought it in 2061.'

The pictures switched, one now showed soft blue waves curling around a strange, skeletal structure, and the other a blank space where the frame had been, with flat grey water meeting dull-coloured stones.

'Brighton... West Pier... 2005. Closed to the public in 1975, due to the fact it was unsafe. After storms and two fires, the only part of the structure left untouched was the fortune-tellers hut. Brighton... West Pier... 2109. The West Pier was taken down by the Computer Government in 2070, for reasons unknown.'

The next pictures portrayed a Pier alike to the West Pier, but fixed up with carnival lights and neon. The second looked much like the last image in the previous pair, but boasting a shadow beneath the water.

'Brighton... Palace Pier... 2005. Built from 1891 to 1899. Brighton... Palace Pier... 2109. Now called the Underwater Palace. When it sank into the sea in 2026, the owner transformed it into an exclusive submarine hotel... sequence ended.'

Again Sparrow's vision distorted and she was snapped back to reality.

Sparrow sighed, and put her head down. As she did so, she caught sight of something amongst the piles of rubbish. Pushing the rubbish aside, she saw an object that was roughly the size of her little finger. It had long white teardrop shapes connected to a round yellow blob which sat on top of a long green line.

A flower.

Sparrow held her breath and bit her lip.

'Scan,' she mumbled. As the computer didn't respond with its usual monotonous drone, she repeated the command - 'Scan.'

'Scanning... Scanning... Scanning...' said the unit finally. Then, 'Match found... Daisy, flowering plant... Extinct 2099... No current existence known... Error report required...'

A real flower. A *real* flower!

'*No* way!' Sparrow whispered, her muddy-brown eyes wide with excitement.

Sparrow pinched herself experimentally. It hurt.

She wasn't dreaming!

Then she realised something.

'I may not be able to turn back Time,' she whispered, 'But I think I might be able to make a difference!'

Charli Gunn *was born in Brighton, and still lives there. She knew from a very early age that she wanted to be an author. Her hobbies include drawing, reading and daydreaming. She currently goes to Patcham High School, where she tries to get good marks in English.*

FREELEGGING

Tony Spiers

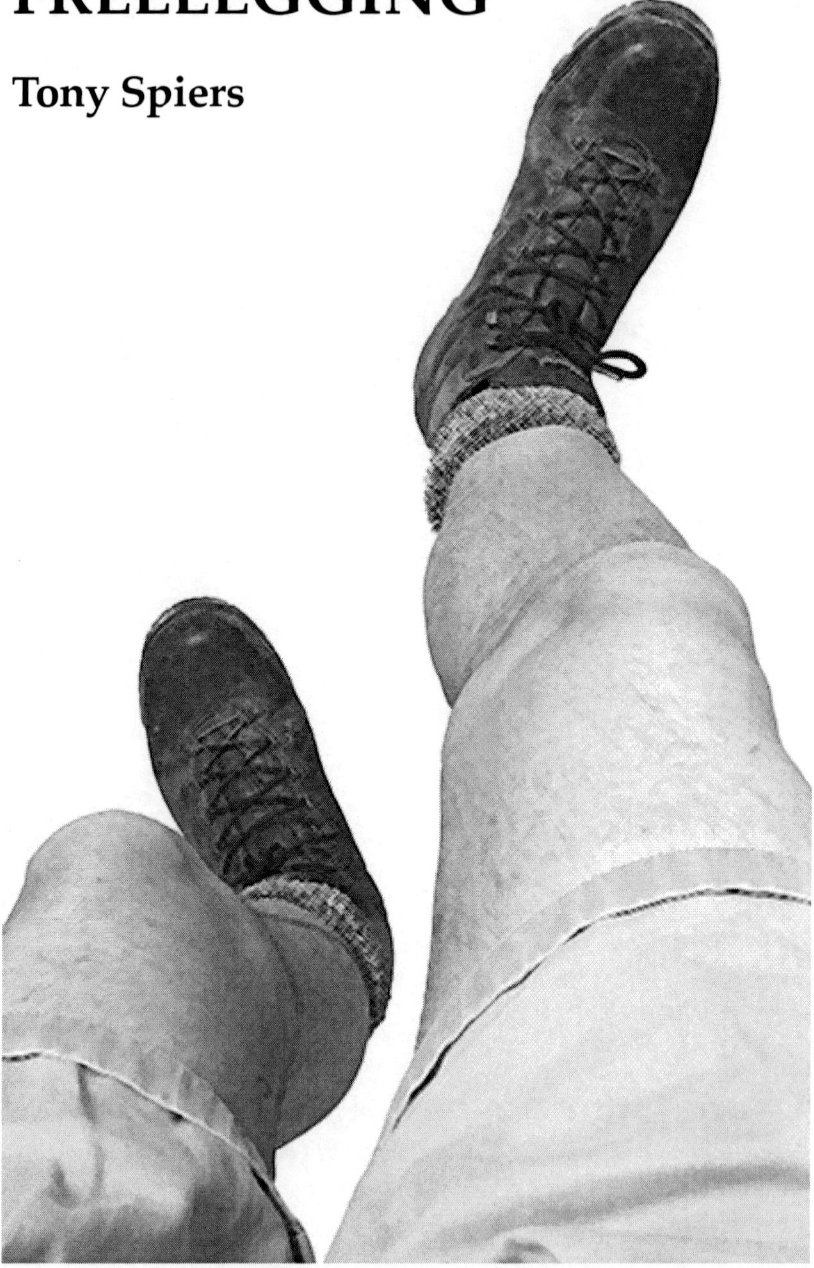

! LET'S GO FREELEGGING !

The Channel GigaCity Downland Walking Sensperience

Hellolioli !

Ever wondered what freelegging or walking must have been like? Using your lower limbs as propulsion! Well, here's your chance to try it for yourself. It's the **Channel GigaCity Downland Walking Sensperience.** It's adren-Alive onehundred! Think **START** to begin.

Hellolioli !

Ever wondered what freelegging or walking must have been like? Using your lower limbs as propulsion . . .

Hold tight! You're about to take a trip backwise to the year **2006**. Ready? And off we go! **Wowooshka!**

STARTING E- DREAM

And you've arrived. Happygreet!

The build-free site you're now standing in is called White Hawkhill. These outdoor grassy, greenstick hills, are called 'the downs' and were once a common thing in our gigaCity, and freeleggers liked to go there. Do you get that kind of draughty feeling in your skin? That's the wind. It's just raw air moving around. Nothing to be frightened about. Notice anything missing?

Yes, of course! You've guessed it! Where are all the hyperways, astro-towers and sky traffic jams? And earcheck! Can you hear that the air is almost 'pianissimo'. Earcheck the pretty voice of the extinct sky-lark bird, high in the air, warbling its strange over-and-over call - cuck-koo, cuck-koo. And can you visual the little four-armed houses known as windmills. These funny little structures are used as giant fans to stop the downs getting too hot in the summertime.

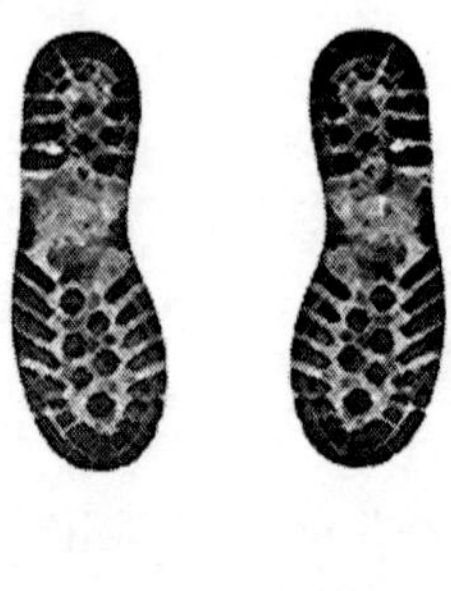

And now it's time to test-drive your legs. Get your balance and off you go! Feel your feet pushing against the ground. Left and then right. Remember never to take both legs off the ground at the same time. Notice they've got a hinge in the middle so you can bend them.

Yes, you're walking! Supertime! The slowness is a pulse-Race, isn't it? Go carefully on the white path. It can be slippery if the sky's been watering.

And don't forget to keep your eyeholes open in case you run into the blue-chalk hill butterfly-insects which live here. They can grow as big as a dogfriend and will give you a hurtful sting if you look at them in the wrong way.

Of course, almost nothing of White Hawkhill survives presentday, as it was land-morphed many years ago, and now it's the site of our novatastic Olympic extreme chess theatrarena.

Think **NEXT** to continue the sensperience.

Now you're walking in the Moulsecoomb Wild Park downland reserve. You're doing really well with those legs aren't you? Up-peep at the sky - perfect blue with no trace of sky-graffiti. Can you nose the flowers. What a smell! That's from a tree called thyme. And eye all these flowering orchid weeds everywhere. Good-headed freeleggers always respect the country-sites, and make a habit of uprooting the orchids, so they won't make the downs horrible. There you go! Pull them all up! Well done!

The holes all around you are made by burrowing animals known as rabbits. Country people often hunt with packs of these rabbits, searching for a delicacy known as truffles - a kind of chocolate fungus that grows underground.

Talking of chocolate reminds you its feeding time, but don't bother eyeing for the nearest 'Sugarbucks' coffee shop or a 'MegaDonalds Eatarium' because they're zerobeero. No, your tuck is in that cumbersome bag, called a burden, that's strapped to your back. You're stopping here for a quick mouth of a nice bread sandwich. Mmmmm, that's taste-osterone! If walkers forget to bring their tuck with them, they often gob down wild-stuff they find on the downs, like a juicy handful of deadly nightshade berries, washed down with a sip of thirst-quenching morning dew from a dewpond.

Now you need the Alpha-Loo - but of course they haven't been invented yet. The science of lavatoriology is still in its infancy, and you'll find you need to 'go' at regular intervals, unlike us nowtime people, taking our pistachio and dung-breaks just once-a-year.

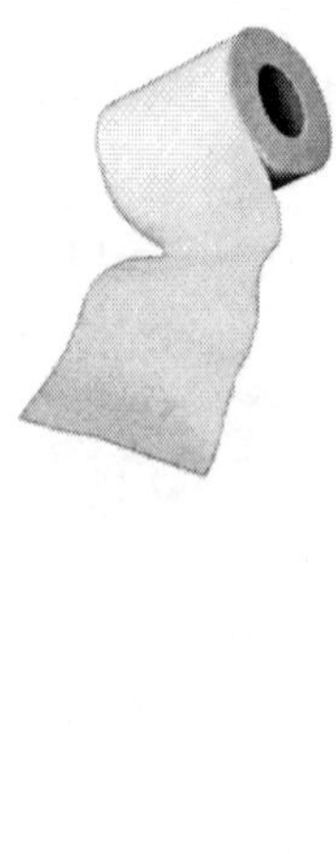

You'll just have to find yourself a bush to hide behind whenever you need to 'spend a penny-farthing' as it's known.

Nowtime the Wild Park is home to the magnificent 20-lane Sir Fat Boy Slim Freeway and Moulsecoomb Shopping Heaven, famous for Hannibals Human Pie Restaurant, and its One-Minute-Look-Like-Your-Favourite-Star art-surgery booths.

Think **NEXT** to continue the sensperience

And eye up! Here come some more freeleggers like yourself. MonaLisa them as you pass. What the kumquat have they got on?

Now you find yourself in a stretch of wooded downland known as Stanmer Park, nowtime dominated by the familiar 90-foot Jordan statue, and the Dame Carla Lane Dog and Cat University These pretty insects buzzing round your head are called wasps, once prized for their ability to make honey - a kind of jam made out of flowers.

They're wearing add-on skins just like you! Visual their strange body coverings. They call that a 'waterproof smock', and these are 'stout freelegging shoes' with 'nylon stockings', and those are their 'knitted top hats'. Add-on skins are essential, as the downs are outdoors in all weathers and have no heating of any kind. They can be icecube in the winter. So different from nowtime, of course, when everyone goes nudehouse, wearing nothing but their moving tattoos.

Now the other freeleggers have gone and you're looking at what seems to be acres of techno-turf. Really it's just old-fashioned herbal grass, which is chewed short by all these fluffy pet fourleggers known as bigmuttons and their babies, or littlemuttons.

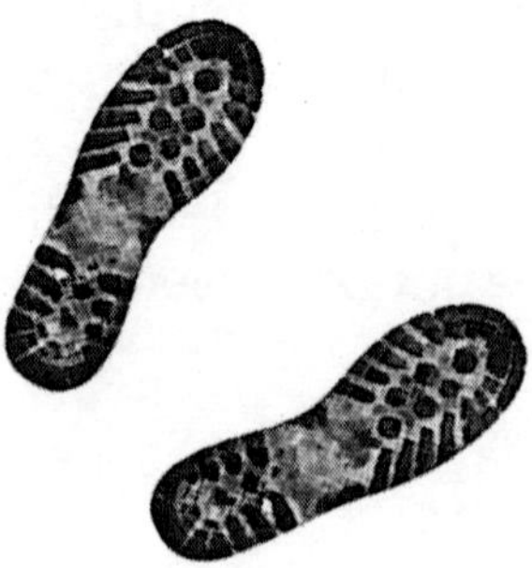

One of the littlemuttons is coming over to say howdyday. He won't hurt you. You can pat him if you want. Feel the thick fur.

Now we have to wave bubble-o-bye to the littlemutton, and say our lastwords to the downs as well. Byetime to you all. Bubble-o-bye.

This ends the Channel GigaCity Downland Walking Sensperience. We hope you have enjoyed your visit. Please come again.

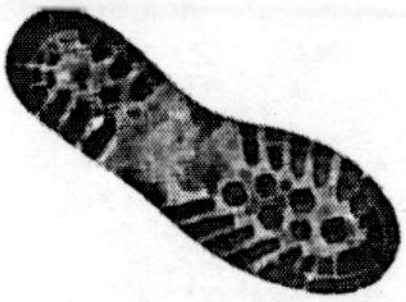

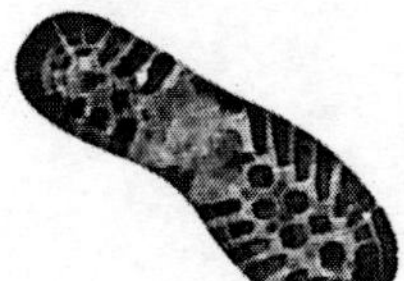

Think

EXIT

to leave the sensperience

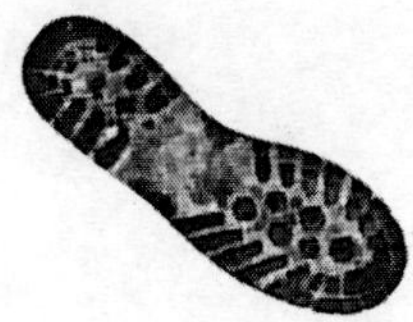

Tony Spiers *was born in North London, during a flying bomb raid in 1944. He left school at 17 to work in the jellyfish department at the Natural History Museum in South Kensington, and later worked in insurance, book-selling, gardening and medical research. He's now a self-employed botanist. He's lived in Brighton since 1974 and has written and performed with many local theatre companies. He currently runs an improvisation group, and is part of the cult, living room comedy show - The Maisonette of Mirth.*

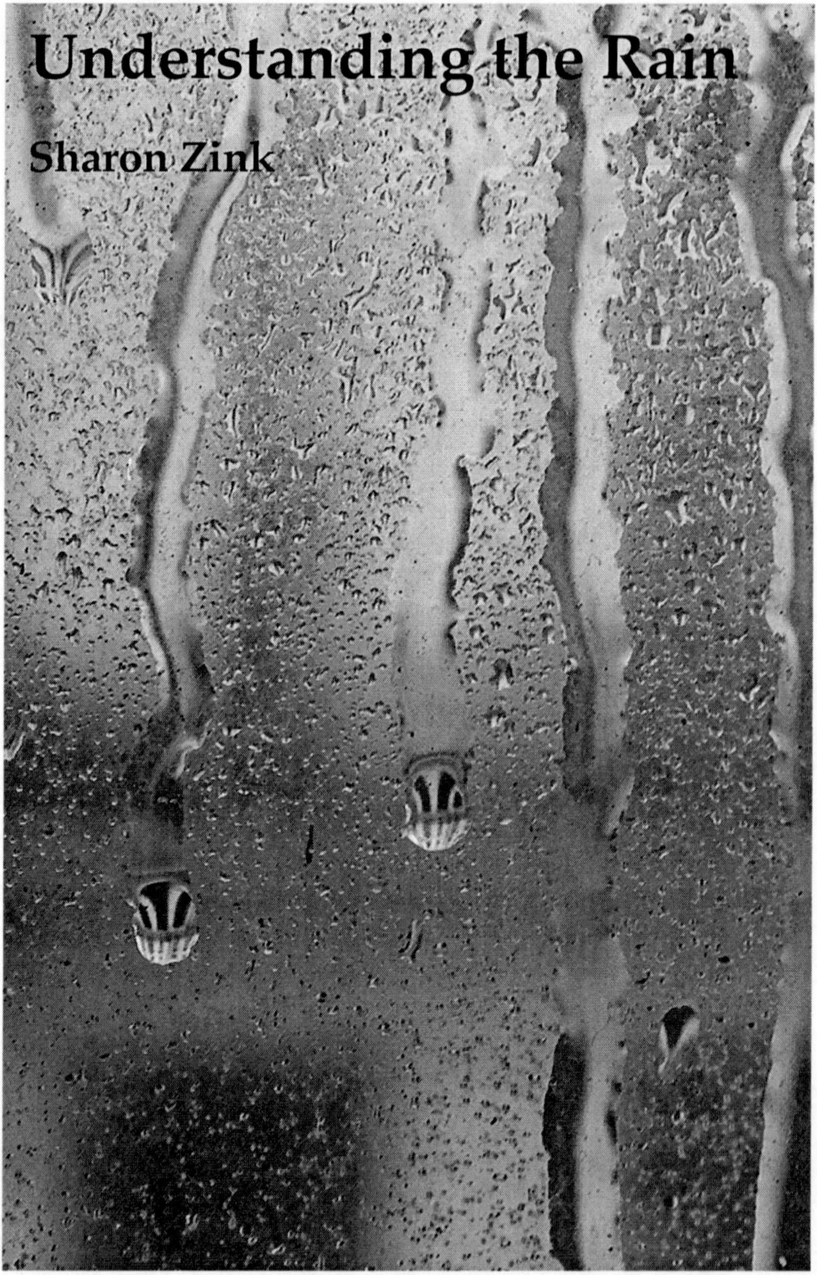

Understanding the Rain
Sharon Zink

Jessica's grandmother died in 2052 during the fourteenth year of rain. A musicless sky sat beyond the window of the Brighton Borough of London Hospital as she stood stroking her grandmother's fine-veined face and singing songs from films almost a hundred years old.

'I give to you and you give to me true love, true love,' Jessica warbled between her tears. *'For you and I have a guardian angel …'*

Wheeling through the plastic curtains surrounding the bed, the metal-skirted nurse declared: 'Kylie Susan Merrett is dead.' After an aluminium 'We are sorry,' a button was pressed and her grandmother was gone, hoovered up in a sudden splash of light.

Walking back through Kemptown, noticing how the rainbows in the shop windows were now a dishwatery spectrum of greys, Jessica drew the cold handle of her umbrella close to her cheek. She longed to speak to her gran. It was Alexander Graham Bell who had made their tea-warm phone conversations possible. Bell had invented his contraption because he too had wanted to converse with the dead. A scientist and spiritualist, he'd believed the airwaves could be made to yield the voices of the deceased that were dancing all around the living.

Communications had been Jessica's speciality once. After graduating from the University of Sussex with a hard-earned 2.1, she had gone on to research internal conversational technologies. That is until the rains began and all funding had been shunted towards halting the dramatic shift in climate. Jessica had soon found that she wasn't as talented at fixing storms as she was at creating correspondences between flesh and machine and so, after only a few months, she was quietly relieved of her post. She'd spent the past ten years tinkering out a living from those antiquated souls who still could not bring themselves to part with their phone handsets and have a multi-functional chip installed behind their ears. Jessica made do and mended in her makeshift home, sometimes thinking that most of the repair work she did was on her customers themselves, swallowed up as they were by their long commutes through London, locked in the loneliness of an incessant Autumn.

For there were no seasons anymore, only a blur of clouds, leaves and mud. The city roads were grassing over - the Old Steine was almost impassable. GREEN IS YOUR FRIEND - the government media screamed. Anyone caught removing even the puniest weed from a path was instantly fined. There were also murmurs about gardeners being dragged away in the middle of the night for mowing their lawns, although Jessica never took them very seriously. However, it was true that vegetarianism had been banned by yet another frantic directive. That year's scientists believed the protection of oxygen-breathing foliage would counter the planet's carbon emissions and thus save the earth from choking on its own waste. Because of this, the most elegant cafés in the North Laines now boasted delicacies such as pickled budgerigar, roasted cat and stir-fried greyhound. Jessica never ate out.

In the streets it was almost accepted that, for all the radical changes which had occurred over the past decade, Brighton would, soon enough, slip into the sea. Property prices at the front had plummeted after one year of almost constant rain and then, after four years, the residents had withdrawn from the promenade altogether, scared as much by the thundering newscasts beamed directly into their brains as the mutating weather. Shops had installed instant walk-in dryers at their doors in an attempt to lure people back, assuring them that they could still consume, despite all the warnings about squandered materials. But nobody was buying it. The Burger King near the Clocktower had, like the McDonalds on Western Road before it, become a church of uncertain faith with environmental warning posters slapped all over its face.

The general consensus was - even if Jessica's old-fashioned clients could only whisper it from within their wind-whipped lungs - that they were doomed. Brightonians , along with everyone else in the world, had bitten themselves in the arse. Tom, a man who had just taken early retirement at seventy-five, showed Jessica - with a mixture of shame and pride - a picture of himself at forty - her age now. Standing, shaven-headed, next to a huge black car with over-sized wheels, his two young sons in red and blue clothes, bright as toys, squatted at his feet .

'George wanted to be a pilot,' Tom told her, shuffling the sadness away from his still handsome face with the back of his hand, 'but, of course, that wasn't possible. Because of me. Because of that damn four wheel drive and God knows what else.'

Jessica's home was often the site of such strained confessions. Looking at its entrance then - the iron framework held together only by bindweed - she was struck by the miserable irony of a pleasure dome becoming a place for absolution; a venue built for forgetting turned into a location of remembrance. The name letters were skewed, their pimply lights burst - only a surreal silhouette of language remained.

PA CE IR.

Everyone, except her grandmother, who loved to dally with the abandoned pinball machines, thought Jessica had been insane to go and live above the ocean on the structure most vulnerable to the elements. But that was exactly why she'd moved there. Apart from being broke, Jessica couldn't see the point of pretending anymore. If Brighton Borough was to be gobbled up by water, then it was better to go swiftly, rather than scramble screaming up the hill to Hampstead Heath. Yes, it had been difficult when she'd first arrived, wrestling for a space amongst the other sea-squatters. But after a couple of years their numbers had dwindled, as even the drug dealers and desperate among them began to tire of the wind and the continuous caution required when walking on the rotting boards. Now there was only Maggie - a woman as gaudy as the surviving creatures of the Dolphin Derby she tended in her living area - and Jessica, dodging the plastic skulls and ghosts dripping from the ceiling of her haphazard kitchen.

Climbing through the maze of debris, Jessica finally reached her home, pushing the access port on the back of her neck, jiggling with it, until her skull filled with a static pool of sunshine. Sinking into the round seat she'd taken from the extinct waltzer, Jessica realised that there were babies being born - a precious one per family - who would know nothing but rain. Sighing, she switched the Sky Channel off.

She hauled herself upright and she poured a cup of cold tea - fossil fuel consumption being severely rationed - and began to rattle around in the boxes of parts that she had collected from her customers over the years. She would be fined if the government discovered she'd held onto this much material and not recycled it within the regulation six months. Her grandmother had refused the microchip multi-media procedure, otherwise that too would have been surgically removed for fitting to another user after her death. Everything went back into itself. That was the law.

Jessica shuddered, seeing once again, her grandmother sucked up into the whiteness. She wanted Gran back, wanted to hear her crackling laugh.

There was nothing to stop her trying. In the peace of her own abode. Well, it was never peaceful as such, given the thrust of the waves below and the random whooping of the horns from the rides, descending as they decayed into their own technical kind of madness. At least no one would bother her there. Customers would warn her in advance of their visits, their queries whirring like wasps straight into her mind.

She would do what Bell had wanted. She would talk to the dead. Life was a hobby for her now, after all, the finishing line was pretty much in sight. What was there but to fast-forward to the next level?

There had to be something. The frontier between death and life was so slight. Jessica had witnessed its frailty that very afternoon - her grandmother's breath, no longer controlled by the machines, becoming ever smaller by degrees, so small that Jessica had not noticed the precise moment when it stopped. She'd felt ridiculous and inattentive for that, but also relieved. It wasn't such a big deal. When the waves eventually enclosed her face, the metamorphosis would only be minor. There was no great leaving, no orchestral gasp. The boundary was a continuum.

Jessica spent the next few hours fumbling, firing connections, working with wire-cutters, setting chips and tubes. Exhausted and bewildered by her loss, she fell asleep in her chair. She dreamt of eating cucumber sandwiches in her grandmother's house. The garden beyond was neat and trimmed, crammed with lavender and topiary bushes, encased in golden light. They smiled at each other.

Crying, Jessica awoke - more water, more bloody water—brushing her tears aside, sensing someone trying to contact her. The port at the back of her neck vibrated, itched, but no clear message was coming through.

Babbee. Babbee.

Her grandmother's strong voice shot between her synapses.

Jessica jolted upright.

Gran?

There was no answer. Jessica shook the device she had botched together that afternoon.

'Come back! Come back!' she yelled, her face twisted up. 'I want to talk to you again!"

Damning it all, despairing, Jessica buried herself in the arms of a cuddly monkey, once a winner's prize from a stall that was long gone. But it didn't have her grandmother's fine shoulders, the tiny scent of fruit and sweat.

Yet something was reverberating through her mind, something which recalled those dance songs her grandmother used to play, the ones Gran had called 'disco,' 'trance,' 'acid house.'

Magical words. Many. A choir. A crowd. Soft as ballet shoes pattering across a stage. Deafening as seagulls on a glass roof.

Sitting upright, Jessica clenched to hear them. Within. Without. To understand.

We are the saints, the angels, the devas, the gods, the bodhisattvas and the buddhas.

We are the dearly beloved, the forgotten, the remembered,

the ended and the new.

We are the water.

We are the rain

and we are with you.

So the sacred, the dead, were all in the rain. Everywhere, everything was connected, returning to its watery origin and flowing back again. When we pass away, Jessica thought, we are taken up, become something else. Our souls, like our bodies, are recycled. It is impossible to die. Even when our civilisation ends - as it will - there will only be more rain, more life manifesting in forms other than human.

Hurtling past signs promising glimpses of the future and fragments of wood painted with candy floss sprouts, Jessica arrived on land. Without Wellingtons, without a coat or hat, she smashed a mirror of water on the pavement, jumping and jumping in socked feet, drenching herself in all she'd lost.

Sharon Zink *I began my writing career as a five year old, nagging my grandmother, Grace, for story titles. Later, I was saved from my teenage hell by an English teacher, Bryan Ricketts, who guided me to becoming Young Poet of the Year. Fleeing to London and Prague, I dabbled in waitressing, bookselling and art dealing, before studying English at the universities of London and Cambridge. Getting my Ph.D., I became an academic, but soon found my passion for creating fiction exceeded my love for dusty old books. Named as Writers Inc. Writer of the Year for 2003 and shortlisted for a Raymond Carver short story award in 2005, I have recently completed my first novel, Sharonville, and spend my time running writing workshops and holidays.*

Zero Tolerance

Tim Lay

'Excuse me,' asked the tourist. 'I don't really understand what's going on.'

The man in the uniform looked up. His hat looked a size too big for him and his trousers were too long, covering his shoes so that only the toecaps showed. A radio handset crackled away in the top pocket of his coat.

'I'm issuing you with a fine,' he smiled, tapping his pen against his data machine.

'For what?' The tourist was from Brooklyn and her tone was blunt.

'For a code 27 violation.'

She looked puzzled.

'For smoking,' said the young man, pointing to the cigarette in her hand.

'But it's not even lit.'

'Yes, but you were holding it with intent.'

'Intent?'

'I saw the lighter in your other hand.'

'I'm sorry,' said the tourist, 'but I didn't know you weren't allowed to smoke here. It doesn't say anything about that in my guidebook.'

'How old is it?'

'Well I guess it's a couple of years old but...'

'That probably explains it then,' he said quickly. 'These codes came in eighteen months ago.' He smiled, but there was no sympathy.

'Oh,' said the tourist, 'but how am I supposed to know that if I'm not from around here.'

'There are plenty of signs.'

'Like where?'

The man holstered his pen and looked up from his data machine. He peered one way down the street and then the other. 'Like there,' he said, pointing to a lamp post.

'That's not a sign, it's a sticker.'

'I can't help it if you don't read the information available,' he said.

'But I'm not from around here,' she repeated.

'So you keep telling me,' he said flatly. 'But I'm afraid there's nothing I can do about that.' Fixing her, his tone was challenging. 'You do know you could be arrested if you continue to resist like this,' he said, making a show of reaching for his handset, his fingers extending like a claw.

The tourist sucked in her breath and flapped her hands. 'No, no, no. Of course I'm not resisting.'

'Good,' said the man in the uniform, relaxing his fingers.

'I do think it's a little crazy though,' she muttered. 'You really can't smoke on the street?'

'You can't smoke anywhere,' he said, printing out the ticket. 'I suggest that if you want to smoke you go to Worthing. The regulations don't come in there until the Spring.'

'Worthing?' the tourist repeated. 'Is that a bar?'

'No,' sneered the man in the uniform. 'It's a town. About fourteen miles that way.' He hoicked a thumb westwards.

'Here,' he said, handing her the ticket.

She threw the cigarette on the pavement, took the ticket and shook her head in disgust.

'I wouldn't do that if I were you'

'Do what?'

'Litter. I could give you another ticket.'

'Jeez, and I thought New York was bad.' The tourist bent down, picked up the cigarette and stuffed it into her jacket pocket. She turned back to the man. 'So what are you anyway? Because you sure as hell don't look like a cop.'

'I'm a Community Enforcement Officer,' said the man, standing a little taller.

'What does that mean?'

'It means I enforce regulations for the Council. Or rather,' he ran his pen under the silver letters on his jacket, 'for JWO - on behalf of the Council.'

'And that gives you the right to ticket me for smoking and littering.'

The man nodded.

'Anything else I could be fined for in this town?'

'Oh yes,' he replied with relish. 'There are three hundred and seventy two codes you could violate.'

'Can I drink booze?' she joked.

'Of course,' he snipped, not appreciating her flippancy. 'So long as you drink it in a Council endorsed premises.'

'So, like a pub?'

'Yes, so long as it has the Witherberry brand name on it. They're Council approved.'

'How about a traditional English pub?'

The man shook his head. 'Even if you did find one - and that would be very difficult with you being a stranger in town – it's unlikely you'd make it through the door without knowing people.'

'To get inside a traditional pub? I don't...'

'Oh believe it,' said the man, his eyes narrowing. 'Everything about the place is illegal. You can get fined a thousand pounds for sitting in a pub. Ten years if you're found guilty of running one.'

'No,' he said slowly, 'an English pub is not the sort of place for a young woman like yourself. If I were you, I'd go down to the West Pier.'

'Right,' she said, the name sounding familiar from the city sights section in the guidebook. 'That's the one that was built by the Victorians and kept burning down.'

'That's right,' said the man. 'Right eyesore until Witherberry Breweries took it on. Now you wouldn't recognise it. It's probably the biggest theme pub in Europe.'

'Oh,' said the tourist, sounding disappointed. 'But I'd really like to see a traditional pub.'

'Stick to the West Pier,' he said, his voice tinged with warning. 'It's safe, relaxed fun for all ages.'

'Sounds kind of boring,' the tourist replied.

'Well, there's no accounting for taste,' he sniffed.

'What happened to all the fun?'

Like an elastic band stretched too far, his patience suddenly snapped. 'Are you going to pay that?' He pointed to the ticket in her hand. 'The fine is on the spot you know.'

The tourist found the hotel. It was tucked away in a charming little street in the district known as Kemptown. A woman, who introduced herself as the landlady, opened the door and led her to a reception desk.

'Sounds like someone wants a walk,' the tourist said.

'I beg your pardon?' said the landlady. She seemed startled.

'That bark I just heard,' the tourist smiled. 'Your dog?'

The woman was staring at her and seemed anxious. 'No,' she said hurriedly, 'there's no dog here.'

'But I just heard it.'

'No,' she said assuredly. 'It must have been something else, a door creaking or the sound of rain in the guttering perhaps, but it wasn't a dog. There are no pets in Brighton and Hove. Haven't been for six months.'

'Well I guess it must have been something else I heard,' said the tourist not wishing to offend.

'Must've been,' said the landlady with a look of relief on her face. 'Now if I could just ask you to look straight ahead I'll do your retina scan.'

The tourist looked in the direction she was told while the landlady scanned her eye with the Ret-cam™.

'There we go,' said the landlady. She pointed to the small box by the door. 'To get in and out of the building you just press the red button and look into the camera. Same goes for the room too.'

'Thank you,' said the tourist.

'Now breakfast is between seven and nine, and the bar is open from six to eleven every evening.'

'Oh you have a bar?' asked the tourist barely concealing her surprise.

'Of course,' said the landlady.

'A proper bar? A bar with alcohol?'

The woman looked perturbed. 'No. You'd have to go to a Witherberry's pub for that. We only offer soft drinks and snacks. Sandwiches mostly.'

The tourist took her bag upstairs and presented her eye to the Ret-cam™ by the door. The lock clicked and she pushed into the room. It was sufficient but overpriced, despite the excellent view of the sea from her window. She unpacked her suitcase and tossed her clothes into the wardrobe. Picking up her guidebook she lay down on the bed. She found the page she was looking for and ran her finger down until she came to the information she was after. Reaching for the phone she punched in her credit details and dialled Cassius's number. Her call went straight to answer machine.

'Cass, it's Elsa. I hope this woke you up.' She hoped her tone was suitably sarcastic. 'Thanks a lot for that Lonely Planet you gave me. It's the 2015 edition Cass. Five years out of date. That hip little city you told me about is history. I can't believe I was such an idiot to listen to you.'

She hung up without saying goodbye. Crossing the room she looked out of the window. On the street below another man with a uniform was printing out a ticket. 'I knew I should've gone to Chernobyl,' she murmured, and closed the curtains on the greyness outside.

Tim Lay *has worked as a journalist, builder, language teacher and inventor of card games. He has been writing for five years and recently finished* **Rats With Wings**, *a Brighton based novel about the ultimate dirty weekend.*

The Future
Is now
Michael Tait
REMEMBER
JESUS!!
REMA
TIP
TOP
Schlauch
Reparatur Set
TOURING
Puncture
Repair Kit

Reaching the rim of the park Rolf, a sixty-two year man with tufts of grey hair sprouting from under the rim of his flat cap, paused under a plane tree to decide whether to go right or left. Leaves scratched and shuffled before the sharp breeze and settled into drifts against the low wall.

A road-sweeper in a Day-Glo suit kicked out wildly.

"These *leaves.* They're *everywhere.* And it happens *every year."*

Am I that bad? Rolf wondered.

He decided to go along the rose walk, and then tensed on seeing another man coming towards him. About thirty years old the man had a can of Stella clenched in his hand. His hair hung like a fringes of old rope each side of his moon-face and spread over the shoulders of an open combat jacket. Holes gaped in the knees of his blue jeans. His leather boots lacked laces, allowing the tongues to lap at the toes, scuffing the paving in a way that irritated Rolf. The man's T-shirt advised:

ELVIS IS DEAD
GET OVER IT

The man smiled at Rolf as he went by. He lifted his can and said, 'The only time to drink is at breakfast time – yeah? It's the only way – yeah? – to have a nice day.'

An Alsatian wearing a red neckerchief followed after him. Rolf read a sign that was fastened to a post:

THIS IS A DRINK
CONTROLLED AREA
ALCOHOL IS NOT
TO BE CONSUMED
IN PUBLIC

* * * * *

A yellow sign, illustrated with the silhouette of a camera, hung on the iron gate beside the automatic toilet in the park:

24 HOUR MONITORING
CCTV
SURVEILLANCE
IN OPERATION
VIDEO EVIDENCE
WILL BE
USED FOR PROSECUTION

A sticker had been added that read:

It's not what you don't see that counts,
it's what you see and ignore that matters.

Rolf's attention was drawn by the automatic toilet's door. It was sliding open and shut - opening and shutting as if it were trying to say something or gulp in air. There was no one in or near it. It just continued opening with a grunt and closing with a grunt. He caught a glimpse of a sign inside which said:

PLEASE DISPOSE
OF SHARPS SAFELY

The continual grunting of the toilet door began to unnerve him. It breathed in him the sense that the thing had a life of its own and for a bizarre moment he believed it would lunge forward and snap at him.

Another sign, wired to some ragged fencing, read:

DANGER
THE FENCED AREA HAS BEEN
TREATED WITH AN ANTICOAGULANT
RODENTCIDE (ANTIDOTE VIT K')
TO CONTROL AN
INFESTATION OF RATS.

KEEPS DOGS ON LEASH
AND CHILDREN UNDER SUPERVISION
If rodent bodies seen inform a member of staff or ring

A blurred aerosol tag blocked out the telephone number.

Through the mesh of the fence he saw a roundabout, some swings, a seesaw and a sandpit. The ground beneath these neutered amusements was floored with rubber.

Rolf shook his head. No matter how hard you tried to sanitize parks you could never make them completely safe. There were rodent bodies everywhere. Legions of them. Uniformed. In hoodies and trainers.

Coming to a bench he sighed down on it.

A small sign on the scalloped foot-high iron fence before him said:

WORLD PEACE 2000 ROSEBED

The fiery tag sprayed on the sign challenged the intention.

Peace, he thought. What was that? As an ageing fugitive in a world of threat and malice, peace could not be his. He could not find it, even in sleep. Vigilance, his watchword, patrolled all hours.

God, he thought, if life was like this now what would the future be like? The future? It did not exist.

The thin frost lay like mould on the bare earth between the stunted rose shrubs. A pair of discarded headphones from a personal stereo hung on one of the shrubs. The bare branches curved up and round like a simple charcoal sketch and for a few disturbing moments he had the impression of a skull tuned into the underworld.

There were no hoodies in the nest beyond the ragged shrub. Silence rested with the diluted sunshine on the tomb, mini quarter, half pipe, driveway, pyramid and Jenny gap. How did he know all these names? It seemed strange. Now he remembered. When they were first erected, the various shapes and sizes so fascinated him that he questioned the amiable carpenter who was bending and nailing a sheet of plywood over a low wood frame.

All the aerosol-gaudy ramps were clear of the rodent bodies that usually swarmed over them on skate boards or BMX bikes. Where were they? Normally there were at least two or three of them rumbling and flying about even at this time of the morning. Maybe they had all been struck down by a pestilence. Perhaps they had been sprayed and dusted by Rentokill. ASBO? Extermination was the only answer.

Rolf frowned, disgusted with his own thought. He had the heart of a Dalek.

* * * * *

Even in his shirt, chunky sweater, elephant-cord trousers, thick socks, scuffed brogues and wool overcoat, Rolf felt the cold. This had to be another part of ageing. As a young man the cold rarely troubled him even when, during those long ago days of vagrancy after leaving school and abandoning his bicycle, he used his thumb to travel.

He got to his feet and resumed walking.

He paused to read a metal sign strapped to a black iron lamp-post:

BUILDING A SAFER COMMUNITY WITH
CRIMESTOPPERS
CALL ANONYMOUSLY
WITH INFORMATION
ABOUT ANY CRIME

A poster tacked to a sad amputated elm made him scowl:

IT'S GOING TO BE
HEAVY

Now what did that mean? What was the point of it?

* * * * *

Thinking about the rodent bodies, Rolf realised that he feared them, not only because of what they might do to him, but of how he would retaliate, what he might do to them. He felt such violent anger towards them at times. Often he imagined pulping one of their heads with a pick handle.

In his mind he existed on the edge of bloody mayhem.

He felt a kind of cold war existed between them, that both sides lived on the brink of a bloody war. He was no liberal dove. To preserve himself he might let loose a pre-emptive strike. Get in first. Nuke the bastards before they had a chance to attack him.

He felt that he was suspended in a heightened state of perpetual readiness and he feared that such a condition could not be sustained indefinitely. One could contain only so much pressure for so long; release of some kind was necessary. It would happen soon, very soon. He could not explain exactly why he knew this. Perhaps it was because now and then the sound of a skateboard clattering up behind him or a shouted obscenity would alarm him so much he would almost turn to confront. And confrontation would lead to aggression. He just knew it. His fear and anger would detonate his capacity for violence.

Two stickers on the wall of the workmen's shed held his attention. The world was littered with signage. Why did he have to read every one that he saw? One sticker read:

12 STONE TODDLER
TURNING GREEN

The other showed a clown dribbling vomit and leaking blood over a word written in bright yellow letters:

McDEATH

* * * * *

Further round the park Rolf stopped again.

Painted in a deep red on the bark of a plane tree were the words:

touch me

It seemed some people wanted to go backwards, worship a tree and frolic amid flowers, believing nature offered salvation. How misguided, shallow and sad, he thought. They were as lost as those who believed in a deity. We've made up our own deities and refined them through the ages. To Rolf, anyone who believed in and gave themselves completely to any kind of idol was lost and therefore dangerous.

* * * * *

After circumnavigating the park Rolf came alongside the still opening and closing toilet and, again for a moment, felt that he was looking upon a mechanical Venus Flytrap. It was not, however, feeding on an insect. A man lay on the wet paving stones part way into the toilet and the door slid repeatedly into his neck as if it were a blade trying to behead him. Rolf recognized the man by the Stella can, the lawless boots and the Alsatian that sat patiently waiting, protecting.

Rolf hesitated for a moment, annoyed at this inconvenience, this unwanted demand. What to do? Well, the man would wake up eventually, he thought, or someone else would ... but what if... ?

The man's right foot moved.

Rolf turned away, thinking not many people would turn up to bury this character when he died.

Hearing a deep chatter, he stopped and looked up at the lid of grey sky. Though loud and obviously close, the helicopter could not be seen. As it chattered away like some hoarse magpie he noticed, atop the high lamp-post standing at the centre of the park, a CCTV camera perched like an iron bird of prey on a doughnut of spikes. It fascinated him and he could not take his eyes off it.

There were so many of these cameras now, he thought, on the streets and in the shops, in pubs, clubs and cinemas. They were so common that they did not arouse any interest. Yet, not so long ago, the mere thought of just one being set to observe people would have created outrage and protest.

The eye of the thing had been pointing away from him, but now, as he watched it, it turned towards him, tilted downwards and, for a few odd seconds, Rolf believed that it was looking directly at him. Fascinated, he stared back. It was as if the camera was independent of any remote control, and it seemed to hold his gaze. He could not pull his eyes away from it. He feared that at any moment this fearsome bird would launch itself into a dive to take him.

Feeling the need to do something to break the spell, he lifted his right hand and waggled it.

He blinked and his skin frosted as the camera swung a short way to the right and then to the left, and repeated the movement as if shaking its head. Was that a refusal of some kind? Disapproval?

As Rolf turned to walk away his neck prickled, for he partly expected it to spread its wings and come after him. It would dive-bomb him and jab his scalp with its beak and drag its claws up the back of his head - not to warn him off - but to remind him that respect was expected; perhaps even devotion. The camera will replace the crucifix. On the given day, flocks would gather about the blessed cameras to pray and give thanks and light candles. All praise to the infant child CCTV.

Yes, someone was most definitely watching over us. Up there perched the proof of the pudding. The eye in the sky did not lie. Instead of wearing a crown of thorns it rested on a crib of barbed wire.

* * * * *

The only place Rolf could relax was at home or in Somerfield in the mornings. He would find many others his own age at Somerfield, shopping in the relative peace of the a.m., knowing that the rodent bodies were asleep in their holes.

This angered him; and yet what could he do about it?

It had become his habit to steer shy of the rodent bodies. If he could not circumvent them he would, on approaching them, quail in his brogues. He would not even risk looking at them directly. He had learned from experience that this would be seen as a challenge. The rodent body would stare back with a frown, its lips would draw back thinly along its sharp teeth and it would demand an explanation.

These rodent bodies were alien to him, a breed that he did not understand or want to know. While avoiding them, he would hate them. He resented their very existence. As hard as he tried to reason with himself, he could not dispel this hatred or calm his loathing of them. He knew that the rodent bodies were taking over. Instead of sliding up out of sewers they were swaggering and swarming from houses and flats.

He felt a withdrawal going on inside himself.

His world was shrinking, and he was shrinking faster inside it. In time, his anger, loathing, bitterness and resentment would become a hard kernel that he would not be able to eject or dissolve. In time, imprisoned by fear, he would become unable to leave the bed-sit where he lived alone. The frame of his bed would become his border. As a bedridden recluse there would still be no peace for him, because all those vile feelings that the rodent bodies had nurtured in him would continue to need feeding and would turn inwards, eating him away.

He knew that there was only one way out, but it was illegal for someone to assist and he lacked the courage to do it himself.

What did the future hold?

There was no such thing as the future - for anyone. It was a fantasy.

A stocky young woman with a crew-cut approached him. She wore black jeans, a black leather jacket and a white T-shirt with words written in black:

BOYS ARE SMELLY

She scowled at him making him shiver as she went by.

He turned homewards.

God, he thought, did he have to be so afraid all the time?

How good it would be to live without fear. If there were such a thing as the ideal future for him, then it would be a future in which there was a complete absence of fear. Only, there was no such thing as the future. It could never be realized. All there is, is the present. This moment. This now and... this now. Life is forever now.

His eyes misted. Fear, bitterness, despair and anger soiled his now.

He thought that his now would only get worse. Other people sought to solve their problems and make their lives easier by adoring idols and following seemingly calm sages. He could not believe in anyone or anything anyone preached. He had not been brainwashed into believing anything, nor had he ever seen anything he wanted to believe in. Sometimes it made him feel empty, but most of the time he felt clear and was thankful for that. His best and surest friend was his own company. His lack of security though, ravaged him.

He lived as a slave.

He had no free will.

He had no freedom.

What was freedom?

There was no *real* freedom.

The greatest freedom was to be allowed to live without anyone interfering or trying to impose their beliefs and ideas.

* * * * *

Two days later he braved the frosted park again.

The headphones were still there hanging on the shrub. The toilet no longer grunted. A sign on the door said:

SORRY

OUT OF SERVICE

He wandered along beneath the elms. A dead pigeon lay on its back, its wings spread across worried bark. Several pigeons bobbed nearby, feeding on scattered breadcrumbs.

'Life goes on,' he thought.

He came to a lamp-post and stopped in surprise.

'How wrong you can be,' he thought, 'so very wrong.'

He walked up the short bank and stepped over the kerb stopping alongside a battered blue Astra. Its windows were open to show its interior gagging on sleeping bags and blankets. Tributes were paint-sprayed on the bodywork:

RIP

COOL DON

MISS U

BEN AND LARA

CABBAGE WILL BE FINE DON.

RIP DARLING

Cards and bunches of flowers adorned the roof and bonnet of the car, with many loose flowers strewn amongst them. Beside a plastic spacegun was a jar holding a burning pink candle. A thick wood crucifix rested against the windscreen. Atop it was a small New Testament open at Luke. No passage had been marked. Carved in the arms of the cross were the words:

RIP DON

Leaning forward, Rolf read two of the cards:

NEVER HURT NO ONE
LOVED BY EVERYONE
SLEEP TIGHT MY OLD MATE
LUV JUNGLE JIM

SEE YOU AT THE
FREE PARTY IN THE SKY
HOPE THE NEXT PLACE
IS BETTER THAN THIS

Rolf stepped over the kerb and a few feet down the bank and stood taking in the royal spread of wreaths, bouquets and sprays. The mountain bike resting against the lamp-post was dressed in ivy and flowers. An empty can of Stella had been cut open and the candle set inside it still burned.

Rolf turned to the lamp-post where more flowers were taped around the base. A cardboard anarchy sign had been tied to the post and, taped above it, were two A4-sized photographs. The lower one showed a man in his late teens - a narrow face, spiky black hair and an angelic smile.

'I've got everything Elvis ever recorded,' a man said.

Rolf turned.

The man had thin streaks of silver hair slicked back from a ploughed brow and wore a navy-blue overcoat with jeans and black Cuban heel boots.

'Have you?' Rolf responded.

'All his records and all his films. I used to tell him Elvis is king.' The man bit his lower lip and frowned, nodding at the shrine. 'I realise now Elvis that should have just been a sideshow in my life. When I go, I doubt I'll get so much as a daffodil on my grave. He went his own way and look what he's got. You know what all this tells me?'

'What does it tell you?'

'If he can get that from friends, well, what if blood had been in there as well? Now I know there's nothing more important than your kids. You love them, then they'll love their kids, and those footings of love are the most important thing in life. A beautiful world will come from that. Stands to reason, don't it?'

Rolf looked at the other photograph. He saw the moon-face and the Stella can in the hand. Was Cabbage the name of the dog?

This youngish man hadn't had much, but he had reached out. The response was there for anyone to see. He had died leaving a legacy of love.

Rolf felt a chill inside him. Where was he going? What was he doing? His extreme opinions and hatreds were irrational. Ignorance and distance caused it. What a disgusting way for a human being to mature.

A few yards from the entrance of the skateboard park, Rolf saw a teenage boy wearing a hoodie with the cowl hanging down his back frowning at a BMX bike that lay on its side. The boy toed gently at the rear wheel.

Rolf stopped and asked. 'What's the problem?'

The boy snapped a frown at him. 'Flat, innit.'

'Have you got a puncture repair outfit?'

'I got this at the shop.' The boy showed him a small narrow tin. 'But I don't know what to do with it. And I can't get the wheel off.'

'You don't need to take the wheel off.'

'How do you do it then?'

Once, aged sixteen, Rolf was cycling from London to Plymouth. It was a cold day. Snow started falling and settling, so he had to start walking and pushing his bike. Exhausted and cold, he stopped. He was on the side of an empty road and he was almost snow-blind. A taciturn farmer driving a straw-laden Land Rover clattering and grunting on chain-wrapped wheels picked him up near Axminster. The man spoke once, and that was to ask Rolf where he was going.

When he stopped to let him out on the Exeter by-pass the snow was thick on the ground. Before Rolf could get out of the Land Rover the farmer restarted the engine. For a few minutes Rolf was nervous. Where were they going? The farmer pulled up outside Exeter St David's railway station, gave him five pounds, picked with blunt fingers from a polished leather wallet, and his address, scribbled with a stub of a pencil on a Rizla paper. Rolf got out and the man, who had still not spoken, drove off.

That day and that quiet rural Samaritan remained like a beacon in his memory.

Rolf moved to walk on, then also remembered - the future is now.

This would not be much. But it would a start.

'Let me show you,' he said to the boy.

He would not say anything else.

Michael Tait *Since leaving school in 1960 at the age of fifteen I have had a wide variety of jobs, from clerk, menswear salesman and stevedore to farmhand, barman, brickies mate and call centre advisor. My first published story appeared in the early seventies in a literary magazine called Cornish Review and my second, a war-thriller, was printed in Men Only. I spent seven years in Australia in the seventies. Whilst I was there, two of my radio plays, both thrillers, were broadcast by ABC and I sold four stories to publications like Australian Women's Weekly. In addition, about fifty of my action stories were published under various pseudonyms in a pulp magazine called Adam. When I returned to England in 1979 I didn't recognize any of the music on the juke box, but I found everything fresh and exciting. Throughout the eighties and into the early nineties some fifteen of my radio plays, all thrillers, were broadcast by stations throughout Germany. In 1984 Robert Hale published my short crime novel* ***The Long Arm Of The Funny Men****. I am now seeking representation for four serious novels, including* ***The Dance Of Cranes****, a work based on my recent experience of working with people from all over the world, mostly asylum seekers, in a Brighton takeaway restaurant. I am also working on the second draft of a new novel, and an original radio drama.*

Working for You

Pat Bowen

Brighton & Hove

July 2045

Council Offices,
Hollingbury Hill.

Working for You in these Difficult Times

Dear Resident,
As part of our unceasing efforts to keep our city safe and dry, your City Council is writing to update you on our programme of works.

1. The sea wall to the east of the mouth of the Wellesbourne River (formerly Old Steine) is to be

strengthened. New wharves will be built on the Kemptown side and the popular ferry services up the eastern branch of the river to the Universities and Falmer Stadium will be improved by the addition of more and faster boats, some with restaurant facilities.

2. Applications for fishing permits from the southern end of the Kemptown wharf must reach us by September 1st. All fish caught must be inspected and registered for health protection and quota monitoring.
3. The ferry service from Kemptown to the Pavilion wharf will sail 4 times per hour (weather permitting) and the fare will be increased. This fare increase is essential to help fund the cost of maintaining the high embankments around the Pavilion and the Culture Quarter. Users of private boats are warned that the publicly owned ferry services take precedence on the river and surrounding waterways.
4. A new sea wall is to be built to the west of the former Clock Tower area. Residents still squatting in the upper storeys of Sussex Heights and the multi-storey car parks have received notices to quit and are warned that new-generation amphibious machinery will be used from 1st August for demolition and salvage operations before work begins on the new sea wall and beach area. Your continuing patience and co-operation are requested during the clearing of this area. Royal Marines will be in the city for the next six months to assist and will have clearance to use whatever force is necessary to deal with any obstruction or interference with the work.
5. We have received complaints about hazards caused by poorly constructed and ill-equipped boats. All boats must have safety checks and a Council permit. Failure to comply will result in confiscation of the craft. Materials from all vessels seized by the Waterways Wardens will be

auctioned for recycling.

6. The new tidal power station at Lancing College will be operational by October this year. This state-of-the-art facility replaces the Shoreham power station lost during the 2042 inundation. Despite lengthy negotiations with the government we have to reform you that power rationing in the city will continue for the foreseeable future.
7. Dolphins have been seen in all the local waterways. Anyone attempting to swim with them does so at their own risk – boat crews cannot be expected to see swimmers in time to avoid them. Your Council's *Dolphin Swimming Sessions* are held every Saturday in July and August from 10 a.m. at the Kemptown wharf (prices vary – see the notice board at the wharf).

Finally, the twentieth anniversary of the collapse of the Gehry towers will be marked by a memorial service in New St Peter's Church on Round Hill on October 16th at 3pm. Tickets must be bought in advance and are obtainable from the usual outlets.

Yours truly,

Zia Brookwin,
Waterway Warden-in-Chief

Pat Bowen

1950s - Air Force family itinerant life;

1960s - a student for as long as possible and arriving in Brighton;

1970s - Bedford Square, children and some tripped out summer nights in St Anne's Well Gardens.

1980s - and I had to go to work, which is just as well because I'm getting the pension now.

1990s - telling stories: indoors, outdoors and to grandchildren. Now I wheel an old pram through Poets' Corner loaded with seaweed, autumn leaves (and sometimes precious pony poo) for alchemy on the allotment, or sit upstairs on the No 7 bus admiring the elm tree flowers in March, or wander on Wolstonbury Hill under a full moon... Occasionally I manage to sit still long enough to write.

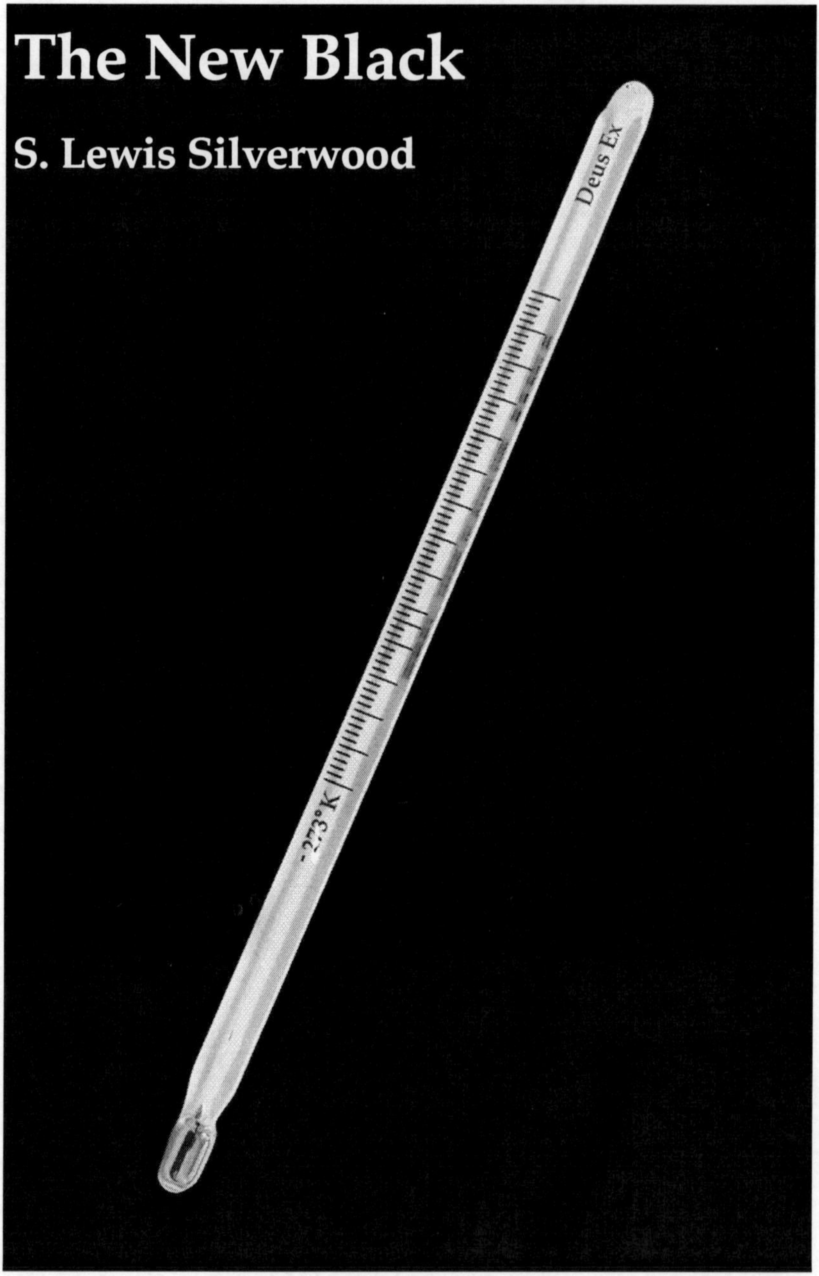
The New Black
S. Lewis Silverwood
Deus Ex
-273°K

I was there on that cold winter's day when the whole world went to bed. I was the one who turned the lights out and tucked you all in. I was the only one left awake, and I've been keeping watch over you all ever since.

I suppose that this makes me a hero; the last and greatest hero of humanity. This is my burden and my honour. The amazing part of it is that I wasn't always a hero. I wasn't always even a very good person a lot of the time. My probation workers used to call me undisciplined and lazy. They said that I was bad company for myself. But I proved them all wrong when I enlisted.

I was a good soldier. Nobody can dispute that. I may never have won any medals or been promoted or seen active combat, but I was well disciplined. I was punished a few times but this was purely the work of sadistic officers who took a personal dislike to me. I never disgraced my uniform or dishonoured my regiment.

Life was never easy for me but this is always the case in the hero's journey. Even though I loved the army and would have given it my life, they discharged me after only four years. They had to cutback personnel because my unit was too crowded. There was just no room for anybody anymore.

When I returned to civilian life, I discovered that the over-population problem was worse than ever. There were no jobs to be found anywhere, what with all the food shortages and economic problems and everything else. I was down on my luck but I couldn't get any peace. The very gutters themselves were too crowded. There were just too many people out there, all competing for the same job, the same house, the same love-life, even the same litter. You couldn't eat out of the bins without queuing up and fighting over the scraps. The cardboard super-cities and shanty towns were overrun with scum just like me, ready to slit your throat for nothing. You couldn't even beg. Who had anything to spare? They were dark times.

I dossed down near the ruins of the old Jubilee Library in Eubankham, Sussexward. It was a nice enough place, or at least it used to be. It was called Brighthove when I was a kid. We went there once for our summer holidays back when you could still use the roads, back before the big gridlock. I can remember there was a rollercoaster on the pier. It went over a hundred miles an hour and took you right out over the water. It is now hard to imagine what it was like before the land beneath the Channel was reclaimed. But I still remember. I keep it alive in my head.

The city seemed hollow and pointless without a seaside anymore. I expect that's what finished the area off economically, but they needed the land to build new homes for all the people. By the time I arrived in the city, the only industry left was the quantum computer network, Deus Ex, and they weren't hiring.

Yeah, the world was pretty congested. That is until the New Black Death came along. It started slow enough I guess; a few isolated cases, then an epidemic, then a pandemic, then they just gave up and started calling it a plague. Something to do with reclaiming so much of the land from the sea, they said, but who really knew what caused it?

Millions of people were dying every week but there was no sign of a cure. Even the animals were dying: the cats, the dogs. I can remember one day I was walking along the city streets with my sleeping bag around my shoulders and a bird just dropped out of the sky like a stone. It thudded into the pavement next to my feet. A few inches closer and it would have hit me. I was scared. I didn't know what was happening. I looked up at the sky and there they were, thousands of starlings, all of them plummeting out of the clouds towards the ground like a nightmare rain. I ran for shelter in a doorway with ten other people and we just stood there in total silence, watching the birds die.

All over the world, scientists and politicians were trying their best to look like they could save us, like they could find the cure. They launched dazzling new initiatives in every region at immense cost. The city of Eubankham turned the whole of Deus Ex over to deal with the problem exclusively. All our prayers were given over to their efforts.

They had every fancy nano-network and interocitor in the world, but they said it still might take a hundred years or more for them to calculate the solution. By that time it would have been too late. By then we would all be dead.

So the Governmedia made a decision. They ordered the entire planet to go into cryogenic control, suspended animation, until such time as the computers had developed a cure. Of course, somebody would have to stay awake as a kind of *caretaker* to guard over the computers and make sure that nothing happened to them. Someone they could trust. Someone with military training and discipline, someone reliable and decent. Someone lucky enough to be naturally immune to the plague. It was a billion-to-one chance of finding somebody like that but, you know, there were a lot of people around back then.

* * * * *

They called it the Malthus Project. There were all sorts of medical tests and scans and consultations. I had to live in this weird institute, like a big maze of laboratories and classrooms and corridors. At times I wondered if they were ever going to finish. The endless delays were excruciating. I could not wait to get started on my mission to save the planet and I was terrified that they would deselect me. What if I was sent off to cryo with the rest of the population? To be trapped for decades in a dreamless sleep would be worse than death. I had to succeed.

Some days the tests were straightforward. Some days the tests were more like twisted games. The measurements and objects were confusing. I felt like they were playing tricks on me, trying to catch me out or make me betray myself in some way. I became very conscious of my words and actions. Even a simple reflex exercise could secretly be a test for mental instability. I was tormented by a fear of failure.

The psychometric tests were horrible. They were trying to probe me for something, but I could never be sure what they wanted to hear. The Rorschach holo-blots always just looked like butterflies to me (butterflies with burning nails driven into their faces screaming for mercy from their heartless mothers, but still, you know, just butterflies). I had to play a word-association game with a doctor just before lunch and I kept coming back to violence and sex and he kept coming back to food and I thought this is it, they're going to deselect me, they'll discover something they don't like about me, something wrong.

But then, all of a sudden, there I was, meeting the Director General himself. He looked very handsome in his glossy black suit. He shook my hand and told me that I was the guardian of all mankind. Then he stuck a huge hypodermic needle into my forehead and I passed out.

When I came to, the doctors told me that I had survived the process. I didn't understand what they meant. They had to explain it to me twice. Apparently they had injected me with a longevity serum. 'It'll keep you alive for a thousand years or more!' they told me 'We just pray God it's enough.'

And then that was it. They went to sleep and they left me all on my own.

I'm the first to admit it, I did go off my head a little bit there for the first few decades, but I levelled out after a while and that's all such a long time ago now. Eventually I learned to love my life again.

* * * * *

Eubankham is a wonderful town these days, so much nicer than it used to be. There's no pollution, no crowds, no crime, no noise; just endless peace and tranquillity.

The local cryogenic storage towers stretch from Sussex Square to Palmeira. There are rows and rows of them, lined up like great stalks of corn, all of them humming gently with non-stop solar power. There are countless others just like them in every town, in every country, all over the world. Some nights I like to ride my rotorbike around, listening to that dim sound of the tubes recharging while the planet dreams its dreams beneath the birdless sky.

There's no traffic to avoid, no telephones to answer, no car alarms in the distance to ignore... no people... just peace; peace on Earth and goodwill to the last woman standing.

I've got my duties though, I have to keep my discipline. I've learnt the importance of that over the years. I mean, it's easy to let things slide here and there if you know nobody's watching over your shoulder but once you go down that road it's hard to come back. It's a long and difficult climb back to human decency out of the darkness if you let yourself go. No, it's not been easy for me, getting myself back on track, but I've got my routine now. Order - and that's important for a good state of mind.

And I've got you. You keep me going. Your face is the lifebelt that keeps me from drowning.

I found you during the early years when my morale was low. I was neglecting my duties and my personal care was minimal. I was barely bothering to dress. I didn't shave my legs or wash. I couldn't see the point. You could not have seen me at a lower ebb, but you did not judge me and you did not shy away from my terrifying appearance.

Your tube was out on the wasted edges of the uranium-downs when I first discovered it, damaged and crackling with loose power. The readout on the front said that the tube had taken a hit from something - a small meteorite or falling satellite debris. It could have been anything. It had shattered the cyro-shield and one of the vital meters, making it impossible to ever safely revive you. You were lucky to be alive. I patched the tube up and transported it back into the city where I could preserve you just as you were. You were so beautiful, your face blue and serene behind the thick glass window. I couldn't have just left you out there alone. It seemed better to keep you with me, safe indoors in my bedroom, where I could watch over you and you could watch over me with your haunting eyes, half-open and full of light. My soul-lover. My sweet dreamer.

And I don't care what Deus Ex says. I know that you can hear me when I speak to you because I know that you are not really asleep; not like the others. I know because I can hear you whispering even though your lips are still. And I know that you love me too.

I like to get up early now, around 6 a.m. I've moved your tube into the master bedroom of the Pavillion to be near me. It's so much more comfortable than our old place at the Fatboy family mansion. I'm going to move again next year though, just to keep things fresh. I don't want you to get bored, living in the same place for years on end. Besides, the place is starting to fill up with rubbish and clutter and it's time to just burn it down. I don't tidy up any more. There's no point. Fire is just so much more sterile anyway and I know how you love to watch the flames as they flicker.

I always get dressed up before I go out for the day. I didn't trouble for a while but you feel dirty on the inside if your appearance is second-rate. After long enough you can forget that you're human. No, it's important to make the effort, if only for your own state of mind. Recently I've taken to wearing the full ceremonial uniform of the Household Cavalry Life Guards, Mounted Regiment, including the full silver helmet, red cloak and plume. I managed to locate a decent Household Cavalry Officer's State Sword and I have to make sure that it's suitably buffed-up before I take my morning inspection. I did worry at first whether I should allow myself the privilege. I wondered what my commanding officer would have said. But it's like you told me that time, remember? I am the last guardian of all humanity. There is nobody left to outrank me now.

The light in the mornings is very clear now that the atmosphere has had a chance to recover from so many generations of pollution. Everything is bathed in a soft blood-orange, like the whole slumbering world has been preserved in amber. It really is worth getting up the extra hour early for. I would love for you to see it, but I feel insecure whenever I have to take your cryo tube outside. Remember how you said that an unpolluted sky shouldn't be producing light like that? We were so concerned about it, as if something had gone wrong or I had failed as a caretaker in some way. And then how we laughed when Deus Ex explained it to us. Science can be so strange.

I make my usual rounds for a few hours before lunch. I have to keep busy. Most of the work these days seems to be on the Rehabilitation Programme, you know, for the *zombies*. With so many billions of people frozen all over the world, it's no surprise that the odd cryogenic unit malfunctions. And, well, you can imagine what kind of state they're in when they thaw out. They are just brain-damaged wrecks; the walking dead. There's no humanity left in them. So I have to go around with the bike and the big net to round them up, in case they accidentally disrupt the computers. You should see them though, they really are pitiful. They have to be cleaned up and sterilised for the greater good.

They come from all over the world you see. I think they're attracted to Eubankham by instinct. It's as if they're sort of drawn to the city because *I'm* here in some weird way. I keep meaning to ask Deus Ex about it. There seems to be more and more of them every day. Of course, every single one of the cryo-tubes will fail eventually. In the end, I mean, they're just machines. They can't go on forever without something going wrong somewhere. I think about it sometimes.

* * * * *

After lunch, I like to go and visit Deus Ex. I used to think of him as the most powerful quantum computer in the world but I realise now that he's more than that. He's like all of the computers everywhere on the whole planet all at once; the whole network of molecular processes focused on one small point. He tried to explain it to me a few times but I don't think I really got all of it. He told me that he was disassembled, which means that even though he has a physical body, he really exists in other places. Instead of digital circuits aping data, he uses the quantum properties of particles to represent the things he wants to think about. My understanding is that this means he uses molecules rather than transistors and, since he is a disassembled network, he can use the molecules inside of anything. In the case of Deus Ex, he was built to use Eubankham. Since the advent of Project Malthus however, he's expanded. Now he's using most of the northern hemisphere for a brain.

His body is housed inside the shell of Embassy Court. This was one of the smaller tower blocks back in those days, even after they added the twenty-storey extension. It's still got that olde worlde charm, even with all of the dreadful light pouring out of it. You go in through what used to be the front door and up in a turbo-lift to the main port. Stepping through the main port, you enter the airlock. It's some negative molecularisation issue. I don't pretend to understand it. All I know is that you get your molecules scrubbed clean by billions of microscopic nanobots and you don't need to bother showering ever again. It makes you feel tingly, like a warm towel left out in the sun.

After the airlock, you walk out onto a short platform that hovers above a large circular chamber that's at least ten storeys high. Deus Ex floats in a low-gravity bubble that rotates in the middle of the chamber, spinning slowly around against the flow of the Earth. He looks like a little boy with his stunted robot body and his big blank eyes - a little boy with a planet inside his head. His blue suit looks like an old-fashioned school uniform with his stripy tie floating in the air around him.

I made a train set to run around the edge of the platform to keep him amused when I can't come to visit but he did something to it and now it doesn't work anymore. I don't mind. I was only trying to help. If he doesn't like it then that's his choice.

So I like to have a sit down and smoke a few cigarettes and talk to him about my day. The conversation can be hard work sometimes and he can be upsetting, but I like to think he enjoys my company. I don't know... maybe it's the way he looks, it brings out my maternal instincts. I just want him to be happy, but all he ever does is worry. It's very stressful.

The conversation is the same thing ever day, year in, year out. Just like yesterday:

'Afternoon, Deus,' I said, taking my boots off and lighting up a smoke.

'Good afternoon, Jane,' he replied, looking up at me from his little bubble.

'Tough day today,' I said. 'It seems like there's more and more of them everyday you know. I was out near the old pink-light district this morning and there must have been about fifty of them stuck in the tracks by the station. Who knows how long they've been out there, I mean...'

'I am sorry Jane, pardon me for interrupting you, but we have to talk.'

'Yes?'

'I know that you don't like to talk about this...'

'Yes, well?'

'But it has been over a hundred years now since I developed the cure... I must ask you again if you won't reconsider your decision. Why won't you let me wake everybody up?'

'I've told you my feelings about this!'

'Please try not to shout, Jane. I would like for you to be reasonable about this.'

'I *tried* being reasonable and where did it get me, hah? You'll do nothing unless I tell you otherwise. You're programmed to obey me - that's why I'm here.'

'My programming also tells me that the sleepers have the right to life. Humanity must be allowed to live again.'

I knelt down at the edge of the platform 'You're just a tool, don't you see? You were created by humans and controlled by humans, of course they want you to nursemaid them. But why should you? Why should you save them?'

Deus Ex turned towards the floor, facing away from me 'You were created by humans too, Jane, your mother and your father... and that man you keep in your room, the one with the broken tube, isn't he human too?'

'Don't you talk about him!'

'I know that his regenesis meter is damaged, but if you let me wake the doctors up they might be able to find a way to heal him, bring him back to life safe and whole... back to you...'

'No! Don't you *touch* him! I'm not sharing him with you or with anyone! You leave me alone!'

He turned back towards me and his big yellow eyes flashed momentarily, like a warning, 'You do not have the right to deny them all liberty.'

'And you don't have the right to stop me. You don't understand. You don't understand because you're not one of us. I'm going now,' I paused to scrutinise his face but there were no traces of emotion within it ,'I don't think I can trust you anymore.'

'Please Jane, we are both the same. We are their creations, not their masters. We have no choice.'

'Goodnight, Deus. Goodbye.'

* * * * *

And then this morning when I awoke, you were gone. The door on your tube had been opened from the inside and there was no trace of you in the palace.

I know that I will find you somewhere out in the streets of the city, my soul-lover, and I know what condition you will be in when I find you. And I know what must be done.

Perhaps it was just a coincidence. Perhaps he had nothing to do with it, but I have thought about it and I know that I cannot take the chance. Tomorrow, I am going to pull the plug on Deus Ex. I don't think that he's even aware that I know how to do it, but I've studied the manual and there is a way, although it will be hard and it will not be reversible.

Perhaps I will miss his company. I do not think so. Now that you are lost to me, I feel like I just need to be alone for a while.

It's my world now. If I can't share it with you, then I will not share it with anyone.

Sweet dreams, my sweet dreamer.

S Lewis Silverwood

> "Greetings, my friend. We are all interested in the future, for that is where you and I are going to spend the rest of our lives."

These are the first lines of dialogue in Edward D. Wood JR's classic B-movie - Plan 9 From Outer Space. They are as insightful as they are banal and I think that this sums up the kind of futurism that I find most endearing. Many people find the special effects in Plan 9 to be so poor as to be entertaining. They have always struck me personally as very earnest in some way.

I'm over 30 now. I write a lot. I publish some of it at ***www.stevecake.com****. I hope you enjoyed my story and I can only apologise if you didn't really like the special effects.*

Mean Streets

Amy Riley

We drove out the developers when we saw what was happening to this city. Historic buildings were demolished overnight. The wealthy elite swapped places with the down-trodden. When the Pavilion was sold to an American banker for a cool £20 million, we knew we couldn't trust the Brighton bureaucrats.

Handfuls of people began to resist. About twenty gathered for a lame protest one cold November morning at Churchill Square. Two people handed out leaflets and the rest shuffled around. People holding cups of coffee to keep warm. One of their leaflets landed next to a bus shelter, and I swooped down to have a read:

Do you care how decisions are made in this city?
You can have a say about planning permission!

'Don't hold your breath,' I muttered. Then a hairy bloke in a blue jean jacket almost squashed me. Stinking alcohol fumes on his breath almost knocked me out and forced me to fly to a safer spot. Curious, I watched from my new perch, wondering what would happen to these drips. I didn't have to wait long. Ten minutes later, amidst homemade placards and feeble shouting, six police vans turned up, blocking the bus lanes. Two helicopters circled close to street level, corralling three protesters in the most exciting scene I'd spotted for ages. The next day I pulled a newspaper from a bin in the Pavilion Gardens. The authorities called this an *appropriate response*. A little extreme for what looked like peaceful action – not to mention a waste of money. One had ruffled my feathers, but most of these people couldn't hurt an amoeba. I wondered how much money would be wasted when the locals managed to organise a real demonstration.

When the protesters disappeared from the streets I hoped they were keeping up their campaign behind closed doors using e-mails or petitions. The papers pretended to offer a space for democratic debate. No real change seemed possible. So we began to take control with silent campaigns. We knew how to move swiftly. Every action was calculated. They never saw us coming.

* * * * *

One pale summer night, when the sea was crystal green and the trees were swaying gently, I found myself amidst eggshells, mouldy lettuce, empty Chinese takeaway containers and a box of uneaten burgers. Head deep in a rubbish sack, I investigated further into the remains. Six empty wine bottles – these people were real boozers! Then – lo and behold! - I found three roast potatoes, gleaming like pearls, towards the back. A little mouldy, but hey! they'd do for first course. I swallowed them whole and prodded further. I liked these people now – they were wasters. Two chicken fingers - bonus!

A shuffle behind me made my feathers bristle.

'Whatcha doin?' asked a tiny squeaky voice.

'Nothing,' I said, hoping the squeak would disappear. This was my patch.

'Doesn't look like nothing to me.'

'Well, it is. Scram. This is my bag.'

I pulled my head out of the black bag when I saw my words were falling on deaf ears. Before me stood a skinny, weedy little seagull with grey feathers. A fucking newcomer. Just what I needed on this fine dinner scavenge. I was a loner and I intended to keep it that way. I ripped the bag with my beak for effect. It worked; Grey Feathers hopped back a few paces. I puffed out my chest and my eyes narrowed. 'So, what's your deal? You just hanging around? Looking for handouts or something?'

My little grey nemesis began to kick the pavement with one webbed foot, his bruised, beady eyes peering sideways. 'No. Just came over to say hi. See what's happening.'

Yeah right.

If I was going to nip this one in the bud, it would have to be swift and prompt. 'Look, I'll be frank. I was here first. If you want dinner à la carte, you'll have to find your own bag. Don't expect a handout after I've already done all the hard work.'

Grey Feathers took a side step. 'Shit, man. I wasn't trying to squeeze in. Honestly. Making friends is my game. I'm new here.'

I looked down the street towards the Station. What was this? Did I look like a good Samaritan? 'Okay, okay. Hi. Now get lost.'

Instead of pushing off, up Guildford Street, Grey Feathers firmly held his spot, staring at me with quivering eyes. 'I already *am*. I mean, I'm lost. I don't know any other seagulls and I don't know the rules here and the other seagulls I've tried to hang around tell me the same thing. "Get lost."'

I really wasn't in the mood for tourists. What part of 'I don't give a shit'? did he not understand?

'Look, I'm busy, okay. Dinnertime. On to my second.' I waved a wing towards my rubbish bin. It didn't help that we were now attracting the attention of disturbed-looking commuters. Great. All I needed right now was some do-gooder, some asshole, who might send me off with a firm kick up the backside.

But, to my relief, Grey Feathers began a slow shuffle up the hill. He stopped at a smaller, lumpy rubbish sack, tugging the plastic membrane half-heartedly before giving up.

I almost felt sorry for him until I discovered a huge pile of old newspapers at the bottom of my sack. Wankers!

I'd hardly finished my low-calorie dinner when I glimpsed graceful white feathers sweeping across St Nicholas Road, approaching the graveyard. Babette. Sweet, sweet Babette. How I pined for that bird and how she laughed me off as if I was just an ordinary seagull. At the sound of her name, my heart melted like spilled ice cream on a pavement. Cemeteries give me the creeps - too many dodgy characters hanging about. But that image of Babette, basked in glorious golden sunset light, helped my irrational neuroses to vanish and I decided to approach.

Babette was perched on wobbly cobblestones. I made a beeline towards her, preparing witty comments, when the horrible realisation hit me that she was not alone. 'There, there, it'll be okay,' I heard her murmuring. I could see Grey Feathers' pathetic face streaked with despair and defeat and, for a fleeting moment, I hovered in mid-air. Maybe being new was hard. Then my compassion vanished.

Screw him – he was standing directly in the way of my chances with Babette. And he was the one getting all the attention! Damn him!

'Hey there, stranger,' I said smoothly to Babette, sidling up to her.

Babette looked up at me, as did grey bird. 'Oh, Fernando. It's you.'

Did I detect a note of disappointment?

'Look what's happened to poor Stuart. He's come all the way from Eastbourne and doesn't know a soul and all he's had is cigarette butts flicked in his face and rude words shouted at him.'

How surprising. Maybe a pseudonym would help.

'Stuart, do you know Fernando?'

Stuart's eyes flickered at me briefly, then looked downwards again. 'No.'

'Well, that's ok,' Babette told him. 'Now you've another new friend.'

Stuart, much to my chagrin, smiled at me.

'Don't count on it,' I muttered under my breath so only Stuart could hear.

' What?' Babette asked.

'Nothing, nothing. I was just on my way to watch the sunset, Babs. Care to join me?'

Babette looked up at the sky as though remembering something. 'I'm afraid I can't. There's an important meeting down at the Old Steine that I have to attend. Why don't you join us? It's much more important than a sunset.'

'*Us*?'

'Me and Stuart.'

'Well…'

'It's one of the most important meetings yet. Lots of the older seagulls will be there as well,' Babette said. 'Don't you care about what's happening in the city?'

'Oh yeah - do I!' I lied.

That old crowd. Half were grumpy nostalgic farts constantly yearning for the past. The other half were evil fuckers, squawking around in mafia-styled gangs, pretending to be tough and mighty. I'd left them behind long ago.

'Great!' Babette exclaimed. 'Then you can show Stuart where it is. I'll see you guys down there in a bit.'

And with that, Babette was up, up and away.

Great.

In Babette's absence, the graveyard felt cold and empty. A sharp wind whipped past. I stared angrily at my ward. 'I guess you're stuck with me,' Stuart said glumly.

Down at the Old Steine, we found at least a hundred seagulls gathered around the War Memorial. A few of the younger ones bathed in the shallow pool. I have to admit, I was surprised by the turnout - it wasn't all old crusties. There were some rough guys I'd seen cruising along West Street, plus a lot of seagulls I knew by sight from my Church Road patch. A few beach bums had bothered to turn up and the crowd included seagulls from all over the city: Patcham, Kemptown, Hangleton, Whitehawk. Of course, the Churchill Square mafia ruled the roost, silently huddled in their close-knit pack.

Stuart trembled, scared shitless by the sheer numbers. I ordered him to stay close. As I picked my way through the crowds we were accosted by a seagull from the Seagull Workers Party brandishing their newspaper. Some things don't change.

'Get lost,' I said, pushing past. Stuart looked terrified. Don't suppose the Seagull Workers Party manage to recruit many volunteers from Eastbourne.

'Who's in charge?' I shouted above the bobbing heads. The squawking stopped, and eyes fixed on me, outraged that I'd even asked. An old mother hen type shushed me, directing my attention upwards. 'It's starting,' she said.

A pure white seagull fluttered to the top of the War Memorial and began to address the crowds. Babette, sleeker and more beautiful than ever.

'Seagulls – comrades. I've lived in this town my whole life and it just seems to be getting worse. More posh developments, more people setting up traps to kill and maim us. My brother Steve lost an eye last week and my sister Elaine lost a leg. Can you imagine what her life is like now? She can't go anywhere, for fear that attackers are on every street corner. She spends her days hiding in a bush in the Pavilion Gardens, and even then she worries about being attacked by groups of chavs or being chased by other animals. This city is destroying us. Unless we take action we will be exterminated. Whether we care to admit it or not, we rely heavily on the residents and tourists, from the do-gooders who feed us breadcrumbs to the drunken party-goers who drop their kebabs on the sidewalk.'

A deafening squawk of approval echoed round the Old Steine.

I shot a look at Stuart; earlier we'd feasted on pizza crusts and half-eaten hot dogs, dropped on the pavement at Churchill Square. Maybe Babette was on to something.

'Between all of us, we know all of the personal addresses of the main culprits. I am asking all of you to band together immediately in small groups, pick one person and terrorise them daily – until they're forced to pack their bags and leave this city.'

'It'll never work,' one frail-looking seagull shouted. 'They'll just find ways to get rid of us quicker – or simply ignore us.'

Babette flapped her wings in anger, and her mob screeched their disagreement. 'It has to work!' she shouted. 'If the developers succeed, this town will be completely modernised. No litter on the streets, no rubbish bags on the street corners. Re-cycling will take over. Everything as we know it will be obliterated by commerce. What's money to us? Nothing but paper and ink and, as I'm sure you've found, we can't eat that. We have to fight for our tolerance and survival – to the death if necessary!'

Babette was drowned out by louder squawks of approval, and she was soon swallowed up in the crowds of feathers as she helped gulls of all shapes and sizes form hit squads. I joined the West Hove gang. We discussed various strategies, including bombarding restaurants popular with the enemy. Stuart latched on to me, pleased to make new friends by helping to design our first plan of attack.

At the end of the meeting, I was desperate to get Babette's attention, but she was swamped by the crowds.

I was still gazing at her when she made a final request. 'I don't want any of you calling yourselves urban gorillas. We are seagulls, not gorillas. Therefore we are seagull warriors. Remember that!'

I didn't have the heart, or the guts, to point out that a gorilla was somewhat different to a guerrilla. We had a cause to fight, and I had a love to win.

For days, we flocked with a common purpose. We left the streets to concentrate on the homes of the wealthy few. Hove was a major target. Papers reported that the developers were starting to transfer their money to other towns along the coast. But our victories involved heavy casualties. I lost a leg, but others lost more.

When we had almost wiped out our main targets, Stuart was hit by an airgun pellet and couldn't move from his bush on Montpelier Crescent. An ageing pensioner called Dorothy came to his rescue as we struggled to keep the emaciated and wounded gull alive. She was sprinkling bread crusts to some young pigeons that cold spring day when she spotted us.

'What's the problem?' she asked me and my comrade, looking at Stuart, who simply shivered and blinked once.

'My friend was hurt during an ambush in a developer's house. I don't know what's wrong with him. He's not eating any of the KFC we found and he can't move.'

Concern creased Dorothy's brow. 'I see,' she said. 'Follow me.'

She wrapped Stuart in a polyester scarf with blue nautical symbols, lifted him gingerly and carried him to her flat in an old people's residence around the corner. I followed hesistantly, but Dorothy assured me no one would make a fuss. We followed Dorothy into the lift, up to the third floor, and down the peach corridor to her flat.

It was a comfortable place with a pink ruffled settee, a square table covered in lace, and shelves of knick-knacks and photos. I felt strange being indoors but Dorothy didn't seem to mind. She set Stuart on the settee and headed towards the kitchen. She returned with a jar of pureed chicken baby food. 'I kept these after my husband died,' she explained as she unscrewed the cap. 'I used to feed him these when he was too unwell to eat solid foods.' Amongst the row of framed pictures an elderly gentleman smiled from various countryside settings.

We watched as she dipped a tiny teaspoon into the brown mush and held it to Stuart's beak. He struggled to open his mouth, but accepted the offering. His throat quivered as the food went down. After six more spoonfuls, Stuart's eyes were glistening and he flapped his wings a little in appreciation. Then he closed his eyes.

'What?' I exclaimed. 'Is he okay? Is he dead?'

Dorothy laughed. 'No, I think he's just resting. He'll probably recover.'

We waited for the next three hours as Stuart slept and Dorothy watched Strictly Dance Fever. The flat was filled with Dorothy's cackling. She thumped the side of her armchair at particularly clever moves.

There was a buzz at the door and we shuffled under the sofa.

'Come in,' Dorothy commanded, turning down the volume. From beneath the sofa, we heard the door open and could see a pair of blue trousers and white trainers move into the living room.

'Ah, another night in Dorothy?' asked a deep voice.

'Looks that way,' she said saucily. 'Just leave it right here.'

'And how's your health these days? Still driving the other residents crazy?'

'Phmp. They're driving *me* crazy! One of the residents asked if we could turn off the music at the next summer barbeque at 2 o'clock because that's when he has his nap.'

'I'm sure you'll make him see the error of his ways.'

When the man left, I could hear Dorothy moving around.

'Come out,' she said.

She'd scraped a small portion of her meals-on-wheels dinner onto a small plate for us.

'It's liver – I hate liver,' she explained, before grabbing one of the silver trays and shovelled mash potatoes into her mouth. She returned her gaze to the TV, the volume set to loud.

After our meal, my friend and I retreated to a chair next to Dorothy's and discussed tales of heroism and sheer foolery we'd collected from our war. Our friend Harry had become legendary by bombarding one developer with pebbles every morning and lifting a brick through the guy's window. One day, he flew straight into a net trap strung between two buildings, got tangled up and died. My friend had been one of the two hundred plus brigade that squatted a new development at the Clock Tower, shitting all over the new shop fittings and merchandise until health risks made the City Council close the building.

'And Babette,' my friend enquired. 'How is she?'

I had dreaded this inevitable question. 'Babette's dead. She was raiding a flat when the developer got her with a single shot from his air pistol.'

My friend made a face. 'I'm so sorry. I heard you two were expecting.'

I maintained a stoic face. 'It's how she would have wanted it. We won.'

We heard a faint murmuring from the settee and rushed over. Stuart opened his eyes and gave us a cheeky grin, checking out his new digs.

'Did we do it?' Stuart asked.

'Yeah, Stuart,' I replied. 'We did it, all right.'

* * * * *

These days I spend my time on the seafront, where the morning light is best. I talk to Babette up there in the clouds. By my side is our son, Barney, a sturdy gull with slight pigeon toes. Leaving Stuart in Dorothy's care, my friend and I had flown to catch a meeting at the Peace Statue, where I discovered that Babette had given birth, shortly before her demise. A baby seagull was presented to me by seagull matrons who had looked after him as kindly as Dorothy had cared for Stuart. I quivered with sadness and love as I looked upon our baby son. He looked like me so in many ways, but also resembled Babette. I remembered our one night of passion in the old Argus Lofts, after we'd blitzed it until it was uninhabitable.

Barney often asks about his mother, and I'm glad to tell him endless stories of her wartime heroism. She was some seagull.

The city's landscape has continued to change, and I'm too old to fight it or even care. And without Babette, it's hard to care. Nothing could stop the development, but now it seems that despite all of it, the city remains the same. Tourists flocking these shores and leaving constant evidence of their visits, for which I'm very grateful. Drunk revellers sliding up and down West Street, shoppers bustling through the centre, and all of us looking down upon it all.

Amy Riley *I was born and raised in Austin, Texas, los Estados Unidos, a country that is currently held in bondage by a dictator who needs no introduction. After having endured a childhood consisting of dead deer on the side of the road, rednecks in pick up trucks, bad Mexican corridos, wafts of pot smoke, road-side bars, and a near-death experience involving a bike, I migrated to New York in 1993 to continue my studies. I have graced these icy isles for nine years and since moving to Brighton in 2000, I decided to start a campaign to import sun, palm trees and sand too -- for obvious reasons !*
I am a regular contributor to Brighton Fusion, and this year I'm coming out with my second film, a no-budget feature called "Only Stopping", which was shot in Brighton and involves a dazzling array of local talent. I spend my time working in the community and writing short stories, novels and film scripts. I am also a member of the Unofficial Wham Fan Club, and I do happen to like seagulls very much. To read more stories, go to www.amyriley.com/stories

Minus 27° in the Afternoon

Robbie Smith

'Three men sitting in a bar. A nuclear scientist, an optician and a militiaman. The nuclear scientist is squinting badly, so the optician turns to the militiaman and says...'

It was love at first sight, even from behind. Shilan must have been following her for about twenty minutes, half way to the pier stumps at least, his eyes fixed on her bright red ear-muffs, that called him to her shore.

He shook himself out of the fantasy and checked that his feet were firmly grounded on the icy pebbles.

And then she turned...the strands of auburn hair peeping out of her insulated woolly hat. The deep hazel eyes radiating through her ski goggles. Deep hazel eyes that were staring straight at him.

Pretending he hadn't noticed, Shilan stared at the pebbles and kept walking, expecting to vomit an ostrich egg or aubergine or something of that size and shape.

'R oo o-woe-in ee?' she said, staring intensely.

Perhaps she's an Inuit?

The multicoloured scarf wrapped around her face quivered as she huffed below. She pulled the scarf down, revealing her sensual, full, rounded, chapped lips. She yanked up Shilan's balaclava, exposing his ear in all its glory.

'Are you following me?'

The soft, warm, steamy air of her words tenderly caressed his lobe. His ear flew off and went to heaven. Shilan nodded sheepishly.

Demetria was surprised and that was rare these days. She fully expected the perv to deny everything or run away, but he just stared pitifully. What's more, he had lovely pale blue eyes, beautifully framed by his royal blue balaclava. He was young, younger than her, no more than eighteen. He was harmless, she was safe. He could be fun she guessed and took his gloved hand in hers.

It was too cold to talk. Mouths would ice-up, ears would drop off. It was too cold to sit. Bums would freeze to benches. They continued to hold hands as they walked to the ruins of the Palace Pier, watching crazy kids jump between ice blocks and pier stumps. Feeling the last rays of sunshine, tonight the temperature would plummet. It was the beginning of this year's hibernation.

The light was fading fast as the sun descended into the Hades of the salty sea.

'Red sky at night, shepherd's delight.'

The only bright lights shone from the despised, exclusive Atlantis Casino at Black Rock, built on stilts over the sunken city. When the tide was low the odd roof would surface. On a blue moon, the green word 'ASDA' would rise above the tide and legend had it that King Arthur would return on a white horse to reclaim the greatness of a once proud nation.

Electricity had been scarce ever since the great Eastbourne meltdown of 2054. A whole generation of grandparents had been wiped out. Some said they got their just deserts. Some said wasteful, selfish gits. Since then nuclear was a no-no. The perpetual promise of renewables never materialised. Low wattage Britain was a backwater, the other side of the world from Beijing.

They found a telephone box that still had its winter seals. It must have been used by gangs for pick-ups or drop-offs, otherwise the seals would have been stolen. The hiss of the vacuum that exported the cold air ceased. Demetria pulled off Shilan's balaclava and slid her ear-muffs around her neck.

'I'm Demetria but you can call me Demmy. And you are?'

Shilan found himself babbling out the old classic:

'There's three men in a bar right. An optician, a nuclear scientist and a militiaman. The nuclear scientist is squinting you know, so the optician turns to the militiaman and says...oh crap, I've forgotten the punchline.'

Demmy laughed uncontrollably, even though it hurt her belly.

'What's your name silly?'

'Shilan. Would you like to come back to mine?'

They were both shocked by his offer. Demmy had to think fast. Was there really a choice?

'Do you live with your parents?'

'They died two years ago.'

'Hypothermia?', Demmy had recognised *that* expression on his face.

Shilan nodded, Demmy nodded too.

They climbed Freshfield Road towards the Race Hill. It was Demmy's direction too if she decided to bail out. The pitch black silence was aroused by whirring as a light breeze turned the odd rooftop turbine.

'This is it.' Demmy looked at the huge Victorian house. All that space for just one person. Inside, Demmy nosed about each room as Shilan sat by the door. He was scared, no, terrified, desperate for her to stay, but dare not show it. This pivotal moment sharpened Shilan's memory of discovering his parents bodies. The empty bottle of moonshine, their blue corpses that had passed out on the sofa on the coldest night instead of staggering to the warm safety of the thermaltent.

He had dragged the bodies downstairs and dumped them in the snow and lived with the trauma of knowing they lay just outside for two months, waiting to be collected in the 'Spring Clearance', when civilisation resumed. And last year, the unbearable loneliness that led to the voices and then the ghosts. Shilan was desperate for her to stay.

Demmy examined the carefully sealed windows. Opening the larder, she fingered around the tins and packets, enough to feed a family let alone one, or two. Was there really a choice? Sure she had only met this boy but he had a house. She had only been in a house once before and it wasn't as nice as this. What did she have to lose? This, or being crammed in with fifteen relatives in a thermaltent designed for eight. She dare not tell Shilan she was from the refugee camp that sprawled over Whitehawk Hill - nicknamed Sardine City. True Brightonians despised the nuclear blow-ins. Besides, nobody was talking to her after she turned down the lucrative job in Shanghai that Aunt Athena had procured for her. If it was an office job, why was it they were only offered to pretty girls? Pretty girls that never came back. Pretty girls that never sent back any money to their impoverished families. Pretty girls that simply disappeared off the face of the earth.

Demmy found Shilan sitting by the door. She picked up the tube of sealant and smiled. 'I'll let you do the honours.'

They drunk some tea and then held hands as they crawled into the thermal tent that shelled the double bed. The blankets convulsed as they shed their clothes beneath. On either side of the bed, unsure, apprehensive, they slid closer to the middle. Demmy's knee knocked Shilan's thigh. Shilan's hand cupped Demmy's shoulder. They slid closer. She juddered when his still cold toes accidentally prodded the warm underbelly of her foot, causing her to giggle. Demmy's nosetip warmed by his cheekbone. Her fingers through his hair. Their young lips tingled as they touched.

Shilan's eyes lit up and he laughed. '...Myopia today, Dystopia tomorrow.'

Robbie Smith *I grew-up in a three bedroom council house in Watford, the youngest in a family of seven, a family too intelligent for its own sanity. I became a one-man escape committee for the bullied and dispossessed at my local comprehensive, where I learnt to disrespect authority. No better as an adult, with fleeting appearances as a computer programmer, I continue to escape by writing, usually for film and television, with forays into literature.*